My Weirdest School #3

Miss Brown Is Upside Down!

Dan Gutman

Pictures by
Jim Paillot

HARPER
An Imprint of HarperCollinsPublishers

To Emma

Library of Congress Cataloging-in-Publication Data

Gutman, Dan.

Miss Brown is upside down! / Dan Gutman ; pictures by Jim Paillot. — First edition.

pages cm. — (My weirdest school ; 3)

Summary: With guidance from Miss Brown, a teacher who is an expert on creativity, the third grade class at Ella Mentry School builds a car and a bridge to compete in a Brain Games competition against Dirk School.

ISBN 978-0-06-228427-3 (pbk.) — ISBN 978-0-06-228428-0 (library)

[1. Schools—Fiction. 2. Teachers—Fiction. 3. Creative ability—Fiction. 4. Contests—Fiction. 5. Humorous stories.] I. Paillot, Jim, illustrator. II. Title.

PZ7.G9846Mjb 2015   2014041202

[Fic]—dc23   CIP

                                                                              AC

Typography by Aurora Parlagreco

15 16 17 18 19 OPM 10 9 8 7 6 5 4 3 2 1

❖

First Edition

Contents

Lightbulb Head

My name is A.J. and I hate being smart.

If you ask me, being smart is dumb. When you're a smart kid, grown-ups expect you to be smart all the time. Then they get all upset when you do something dumb. But when you're a dumb kid, grown-ups expect you to be dumb all the time. Then when you do something dumb, it's no big deal. But when you do something smart, they act like you're a *genius*.

That's why my friends and I act dumb all the time. We want to lower the expectations of grown-ups. That's the first rule of being a kid.

It was Monday morning. We were in Mr. Cooper's class, arguing about which one of us is the dumbest.

"I'm dumber than you are," said Michael, who never ties his shoes.

"I'm dumber than both of you," said Ryan, who will eat anything, even stuff that isn't food.

"I'm the dumbest kid in the history of the world," said Neil, who we call the nude kid even though he wears clothes.

"I was dumb before any of you dumbheads were even *born*," said Alexia, this girl who rides a skateboard all the time.

We had to end the discussion. You'll never believe in a million hundred years who ran into the door at that moment.

Nobody! Why would you run into a door? That would be *really* dumb. But you'll never believe who ran into the door*way*.

It was Mr. Klutz, our principal! He has no hair on his head at all. But he did have a hat on his head, and on top of the hat was a big lightbulb.

That was weird. Mr. Klutz's bald head

already looks like a lightbulb. So he really doesn't need a lightbulb hat.

"Can anyone guess why there's a lightbulb over my head this morning?" asked Mr. Klutz.

"Because it didn't fit in your pocket?" I asked.

"A.J., you need to raise your hand," said Mr. Cooper. "Don't just blurt things out."*

Andrea Young, this annoying girl with curly brown hair, was waving her hand in the air like she had to go to the bathroom really badly. Andrea keeps a dictionary on her desk so she can look up words and

---

*Who decided we have to raise our hand before we can say anything? That makes no sense at all.

4

show everybody how smart she is. Of course, Mr. Klutz called on her.

"A lightbulb over your head means you have a good idea," she said.

"That's right, Andrea!" said Mr. Cooper.

Andrea smiled the smile that she smiles to let everybody know that she knows something nobody else knows. Why can't a truck full of lightbulbs fall on her head?

"Do you want to hear what my good idea is?" asked Mr. Klutz.

"Yes!" said all the girls.

"No!" said all the boys.

I didn't want to hear Mr. Klutz's idea. Usually, when he has an idea, that means we have to learn stuff. Learning stuff is boring. If I was principal of a school, nobody would ever have to learn anything. I would let the kids have recess all day long.

But you probably want to know what

Mr. Klutz's genius idea was.

Well, I'm not gonna tell you.

Okay, okay, I'll tell you. But you have to read the next chapter. So nah-nah-nah boo-boo on you.

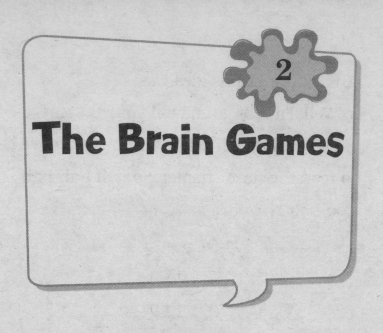

The Brain Games

"We're starting an exciting new program!" Mr. Klutz told us.

All the girls started whispering to each other and rubbing their hands together, as if we were going to get ice cream or something.

"You're going to participate in the Brain

Games!" said Mr. Klutz.

The Brain Games? I didn't like the sound of that. I hate using my brains. Using your brains means thinking. And thinking means learning. And learning isn't fun.

That's when the weirdest thing in the history of the world happened.

A lady walked into our classroom.

Well, that's not the weird part, because ladies walk into our classroom all the time.

The weird part was that the lady walked into our classroom on her *hands*!

"I'm going to let Miss Brown explain the Brain Games to you," said Mr. Klutz.

"Miss Brown is upside down!" I shouted.*

"You need to raise your hand, A.J.," said Mr. Cooper.

Then Miss Brown jumped up so she was on her feet like a normal person.

"You're probably wondering why I was walking on my hands," she said. "*Anybody* can walk

---

*Hey, that would make a good book title!

on their feet. It's more creative to walk on your hands."

"Miss Brown is an expert on creativity," said Mr. Klutz. "She's going to be your coach for the Brain Games."

"The Brain Games are a competition where you use your brains," said Miss Brown. "It involves creative projects blah blah blah think differently blah blah blah create and explore blah blah blah . . ."

What a snoozefest. I had no idea what she was talking about.

"When I say 'up,' I want you to think 'down,'" said Miss Brown. "When I say 'in,' I want you to think 'out.'"

"This isn't going to be one of those

boring educational activities, is it?" asked Mr. Cooper.

Ewww, Mr. Cooper said the *E* word!

"Oh no, the Brain Games are going to be *fun*!" said Miss Brown. "The kids are going to create their own vehicle, and they're going to build a bridge, too. Doesn't that sound like fun?"

"Yes!" shouted all the girls.

"No!" shouted all the boys.

"The Brain Games are sponsored by the Jiggly gelatin company," said Miss Brown. "I'm sure you've all tasted Jiggly at home."

"It jiggles, so you know it's good," added Mr. Klutz.

I've tasted Jiggly gelatin. It looks like Jell-O, but it tastes horrible. My mother gave Jiggly to me one time when I was sick. It was worse than the medicine.

"And here's the *big* news," said Mr. Klutz. "Your class is going to compete against *another* school to see which third grade will be the Brain Games champion of our town."

"Which school?" we all asked.

"Dirk School," said Mr. Klutz.

WHAT?! No! Not Dirk School! Dirk School is on the other side of town. That's where the really smart kids go. We call it Dork School.

I didn't like the whole idea of the Brain Games. I guess I was making a mean face.

"What's the matter, A.J.?" asked Mr. Cooper.

"The Brain Games sound like a way to trick dumb kids into being smart," I said.

"There's no way we can beat those Dirk jerks anyway," said Ryan.

"Yeah, they're *way* too smart," said Michael.

"You kids are smart, too," said Mr. Klutz, "and I think you can win. Oh, by the way, there will be a prize for the school that wins the Brain Games."

"A prize?" asked Andrea.

"A prize?" asked Emily, a big crybaby who says everything Andrea says.

"A prize?" asked Alexia.

In case you were wondering, everybody was saying "a prize?"

"The school that wins the Brain Games," said Mr. Klutz, "will get a trip to Pizza-World Water Park!"

"WOW!" we all said, which is "MOM" upside down.

PizzaWorld is the coolest water park in the history of water parks. You get to go down a water slide on a giant slice of pizza. They have a tomato sauce log flume. The best ride is Cheese Mountain, a roller coaster

on a
moun-
tain made
of cheese. And in
the snack bar you get
all the pizza you can eat.

"We need to choose a team captain," said Miss Brown. "Are any of you in the gifted and talented program?"

Andrea's hand shot up in the air.

"Aren't you in the G and T program, too, A.J.?" asked Mr. Cooper.

I slinked down in my seat. I never wanted to be in the gifted and talented program. That's for dorks like Andrea. But Ms. Coco, our gifted and talented teacher, forced me into it.

"Okay, A.J. and Andrea will be the co-captains of your Brain Games team," said Mr. Cooper.

"Ooooo!" Ryan said. "A.J. and Andrea are cocaptains. They must be in *love*!"

"When are you gonna get married?" asked Michael.

If those guys weren't my best friends, I would hate them.

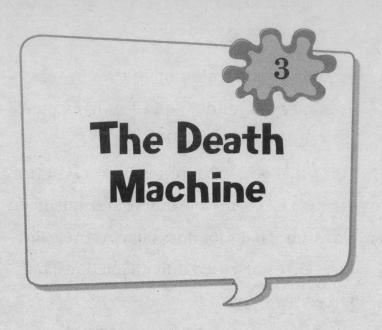

The Death Machine

The next morning, right after we pledged the allegiance, Miss Brown came into our classroom. This time she wasn't walking on her hands. She was on a pogo stick!

"Anybody can walk on their hands," she told us. "It's more creative to hop."

"The students are very excited about the Brain Games," said Mr. Cooper. "When do we begin?"

"Right now!" Miss Brown replied. "The most important part of the Brain Games is building our car. So we should work on that first."

WHAT?! Building our car? Is she out of her mind?

"We can't build a car!" said Ryan.

"We can't build a car!" said Michael.

"We can't build a car!" said Neil.

In case you were wondering, everybody was saying that we couldn't build a car.

"Sure you can!" said Miss Brown. "You just have to use your creativity."

"But a car needs a motor," said Andrea. "How can we build a car without a motor?"

"Hmmm," said Miss Brown. "We need to

find something that will turn the wheels. So what turns around?"

"A screwdriver," said Neil.

"An eggbeater!" shouted Emily.

"A drill!" yelled Alexia.

Kids were shouting out all kinds of things that turn. I looked around the room. That's when I got the greatest idea

in the history of the world.

"A pencil sharpener!" I shouted.

Everybody looked at me like I was crazy.

"A pencil sharpener turns around," I said.

"But how can a pencil sharpener power a car?" asked Ryan.

"It can if it's an *electric* pencil sharpener," I told them.

Everybody looked at me some more.

"Wait a minute!" Andrea said. "Arlo's right! Remember that remote control pencil sharpener that Mrs. Yonkers showed us?"

"Oh, yeah!" everybody said.

Our computer teacher, Mrs. Yonkers,

has a thing for remote controls. She uses a remote control for everything. She even has a remote control remote control. That's a remote control you use when you're too lazy to get your regular remote control. You just press a button on the remote control remote control and you can control your remote control remotely.*

Mr. Cooper went down the hall to talk to Mrs. Yonkers. They came back with the remote control pencil sharpener she invented. It made it possible to sharpen a pencil from ten feet away.

"We can use the motor from the pencil

—————————————————

*Do you know where lost remote controls go? To a remote location.

22

sharpener to turn the wheels of our car," I explained, "and then we can move the car with the remote control."

I should get the Nobel Prize for that idea. That's a prize they give to people who don't have bells.

While Mrs. Yonkers helped us take the motor out of the pencil sharpener, Mr. Cooper got on the intercom and called a few of the other teachers. Miss Small, our gym teacher, came in with four tennis balls we could use as the wheels for our car. Miss Lazar, our custodian, brought up some wood, screws, and tools so we could build the body of our car. Mr. Docker, our science teacher, helped us figure out a way to steer our car. Ms. Hannah, our art teacher, brought up some paint so we could decorate our car.

We spent all morning working. Mr. Cooper said we could skip reading, writing, and math for the morning because everybody was doing such a good job.

Finally, just before lunch, the car was done. We all stood back to look at it.

"Wow," I said. "This car is cool!"

"You kids are so creative!" said Miss Brown.

"We should give the car a name," suggested Ryan.

Everybody started shouting out names.

"The Love Bug!"

"Super Car!"

"Floyd!"

"The Death Machine!"

Miss Brown said we should vote on it.

She had us raise our hands to vote. There was an equal number of boys and girls in the class. All the boys voted for the "Death Machine." The girls voted for the "Love Bug." Only one girl didn't vote. It was Alexia. So she had the deciding vote.

"Which name do you vote for, Alexia?" asked Miss Brown.

"Vote for the Love Bug!" shouted all the girls.

"Vote for the Death Machine!" shouted all the boys.

Alexia didn't know what to say. She didn't know what to do. She had to think fast.

"I vote for . . . ," she finally said, ". . . the Death Machine."

"Yeah!" shouted all the boys.

And that's how our car came to be called the Death Machine.

"You know what would be really cool?" I said. "We should put a rocket launcher on the roof of the Death Machine."

"What's the point of that?" Andrea asked, rolling her eyes. "Cars don't have rocket launchers."

"Rocket launchers are cool," I told Andrea. "Every car should have a rocket launcher on the roof."

"I got a model rocket kit for my birthday," said Neil. "It would be easy to attach a rocket launcher to the roof of the Death Machine."

"Anybody can build a car with no

rocket launcher on the roof," said Ryan. "But putting a rocket launcher on the roof is creative. Right, Miss Brown?"

We all looked at Miss Brown. She thought it over without saying anything for a million hundred seconds.

"I think putting a rocket launcher on the roof of the Death Machine is a great idea!" she said.

Ha! Nah-nah-nah boo-boo on Andrea! She lost two arguments in a row.

"I'll bring my rocket launcher to school tomorrow," said Neil.

"In the meantime, we need to test the car," said Miss Brown.

Neil put the Death Machine on the floor.

I picked up the remote control. Michael and Ryan moved some desks out of the way to make room.

"Okay, let it rip, A.J.," said Miss Brown.

I pushed the ON button. The car made a sound like a pencil sharpener. Then it started moving slowly.

"It works!" Neil shouted.

"See if it can turn left, A.J.," said Miss Brown.

I steered the car to the left.

"The Death Machine is hard to control," I said.

"See if it can turn right, A.J.," said Miss Brown.

"I'm trying . . . ," I said.

It wasn't easy. I kept pushing the buttons, but the Death Machine seemed to go wherever it wanted.

Suddenly, it started moving back and forth really fast.

Then it started driving around in crazy
circles!

"I can't control it!" I shouted.

Kids were diving to get out of the way!

"Run for your lives!" yelled Neil.

Everybody started yelling and screaming and shrieking and hooting and
hollering and freaking out.

That's when Emily tripped and fell. The
Death Machine was coming straight at
her!

"Help!" Emily shouted just before the
car crashed into her.

She was on the floor, freaking out. Then
she got up and went running out of the
room.

What a crybaby! All she did was get run
over by a car.

I guess we need to do some more tests
on the Death Machine.

The Bridge of Love

Right after we pledged the allegiance the next morning, Miss Brown came into our classroom. This time she wasn't hopping on a pogo stick. She climbed in through the window!

"Anybody can use a door," she told us. "It's more creative to climb in the window."

Miss Brown is weird.

Neil brought his model rocket launcher from home, and we attached it to the roof of the Death Machine. It looked cool.

"What's our next Brain Games task?" asked Mr. Cooper.

"Today we're going to build a bridge," she replied. "The bridge that can support the most weight will be the winning bridge in the Brain Games."

"How are we going to build a bridge?" asked Alexia. "We're just kids."

"You have to use

your creativity," said Miss Brown. "Now, what material could be used to build a bridge?"

"We should use something really strong," Andrea said. "Like bricks."

"According to the rules," said Miss Brown, "we're not allowed to use bricks. Besides, *anybody* can build a bridge with bricks. We have to use our creativity and build our bridge out of something you might find in a classroom."

We all looked around.

"Pencils!" shouted Michael.

"Glue sticks!" shouted Ryan.

"Paper!" shouted Neil.

Everybody was yelling stuff. I looked

around the classroom. There was a box of toothpicks on Mr. Cooper's desk.

"Toothpicks!" I shouted.

Everybody looked at me like I was crazy. Everybody except Miss Brown.

"That's a great idea, A.J.!" she hollered. "We can build our bridge out of lots of toothpicks!"

Wow, that was my second great idea in two days! No wonder I was in the gifted and talented program.

Mr. Cooper called Ms. Hannah in the art room, and a few minutes later she came in with a bunch more toothpicks in little boxes. We spent all morning gluing them together to build our toothpick bridge.

Finally, just before lunch, the bridge was finished.

"Wow," I said. "This bridge is cool!"

"You kids are so creative!" said Miss Brown.

"We should give the bridge a name," suggested Ryan. "How about the Bridge of Death?"

"Yeah!" agreed all the boys.

"You already got to name the car," complained Andrea. "The girls should get to

name the bridge. That's only fair. I say we should call it the Bridge of Love."

Ugh, disgusting! Andrea said the *L* word!

"I agree with Andrea," said Emily, who always agrees with Andrea.

"Andrea is right," said Miss Brown. "The girls should get to name the bridge."

"Yeah!" shouted all the girls.

And that's how our bridge came to be called the Bridge of Love.

"Next we have to see how much weight our bridge can hold," said Miss Brown. "We'll do that after lunch when the glue has dried. Who's the lightest person in the class?"

Nobody knew who was the lightest

person in the class. So Miss Brown called our nurse, Mrs. Cooney, on the intercom. She has a scale in the nurse's office, and Mrs. Cooney said we could come down there and weigh ourselves.

After lunch we went to Mrs. Cooney's office. Each of us got on the scale, and Mrs. Cooney called out the numbers. I weighed sixty-six pounds. Michael weighed sixty-nine pounds. Ryan weighed fifty-eight pounds. The lightest person in the class was Emily. She weighed fifty-one pounds.

"Emily," said Miss Brown. "When we go back to the classroom, will you please stand on the Bridge of Love to see if it can support your weight?"

"I'm scared!" said Emily, who's scared of everything.

"It will be fine, Emily," said Andrea. "The Bridge of Love is really strong."

Emily looked all scared as we walked back to our classroom. When we got there, she put one foot on the Bridge of Love, really carefully. It seemed to hold her up, so she put her other foot on the bridge.

"See?" said Miss Brown. "The bridge is holding you up, Emily! It just goes to show that we don't need bricks to build a strong structure."

That's when the most amazing thing in the history of the world happened.

The Bridge of Love collapsed!

Emily fell down!

Toothpicks went flying everywhere!

Emily was on the floor, freaking out. Her hair was full of toothpicks and glue. She went running out of the room.

Sheesh, get a grip! All she did was fall through a bridge.

I think we need to do a little more work on the Bridge of Love.

Welcome to the Brain Games

Finally, after a week, we were ready for the Brain Games. We fixed the Death Machine (complete with rocket launcher) so it was easier to steer. We rebuilt the Bridge of Love so Emily could stand on it without crushing it. The only thing we had to worry about was the general knowledge part of the Brain Games.

"Don't worry," said Andrea. "I memorized the dictionary and the encyclopedia."

The Brain Games were held on Friday night. We had to hold them at Dirk School because their auditorium has a bigger stage. We loaded up our props and rode a bus over to Dirk.

When we pulled up to the front of the school, guess who was standing there? It was Morgan Brocklebank. She's this third-grade girl who is the star of the Dirk School TV station. She does their morning announcements every day.

"Well, well, well," Morgan Brocklebank said when she saw us get off the bus. "If it isn't the kids from Ella Mentry School. Are you ready to lose?"

"Your face is gonna lose!" I said, pointing my finger at her.

"Oh, yeah?" Morgan Brocklebank replied. "I don't *think* so. We're going to PizzaWorld."

"You're going to LoserLand!" Ryan told her.

Miss Brown got between us and Morgan Brocklebank.

"Enough of that," she warned.

I had never been to Dirk School before. It was big. We had to walk a million hundred miles to the auditorium. When we got there, all the seats were filled. Besides the Dirk students, it looked like their parents, grandparents, nephews, nieces, aunts, and uncles were there. Our parents were in the audience, too, but there were only a few of them.

"It looks like Dork School has home-field advantage," Alexia said.

"Don't worry about it," Miss Brown assured us. "You're going to do fine."

When our team and the Dirk team got up onstage, everybody clapped their hands.* Then some guy climbed up onstage. I recognized him right away. It was Dr. Carbles, the president of the Board of Education.

I used to think Mr. Klutz was important, like he was the king of the school. But if Mr. Klutz is the king of the school, then Dr. Carbles is the king of the *world*. He probably sits on a throne and has servants fan him with feathers. I saw that in a movie once.

"Welcome to the Brain Games," Dr. Carbles said into the microphone. "This

---

*Well, what else would they clap? Clapping your feet would be weird.

46

competition is sponsored by the Jiggly gelatin company. It jiggles, so you know it's good."

Dr. Carbles introduced Mr. Klutz and Mr. Wilson, who is the principal of Dirk School. They got up onstage and shook hands. I remembered that Dr. Carbles and Mr. Klutz went to high school together, so they've known each other for a long time.

"On the left we have the third-grade students from Ella Mentry School," said Dr. Carbles.

Our parents clapped and cheered.

"And on the right we have the third-grade students from Dirk School," said Dr. Carbles.

The whole audience yelled and screamed

and shrieked and hooted and hollered. I looked across the stage at Morgan Brocklebank. She was giving me the evil eye.

"Round one of the Brain Games will be a test of general knowledge," said Dr. Carbles. "But first, a few short words from our sponsor . . ."

It's So Jiggly!

The lights were dimmed, and a giant video screen came down in the middle of the stage. Then this man and lady appeared on the screen. They were way too smiley.

"Do you like eating things?" the man asked. "Who doesn't, right? If we didn't eat things, we'd die."

"And do you like drinking liquids?" the

lady asked. "Everybody does. In fact, if we didn't drink liquids, we would die."

"The only thing better than eating and drinking," said the man, "is when you can eat and drink at the same time!"

"That's why our whole family loves Jiggly gelatin," said the lady. "It's a complete meal in a bowl."

"Jiggly has all the essential vitamins and nutrients you need for a healthy lifestyle," said the man. "It contains no sugar, no fat, and no cholesterol. It helps you lose weight, sleep better, see better, look younger, and grow hair; and Jiggly even cures all major diseases."

"Not only that, but Jiggly comes in all the colors of the rainbow, and it tastes great!" said the lady. "But the best part is, it's fun to eat because it jiggles! Right, kids?"

The camera pulled back to show three kids sitting on the floor.

"Right!" the kids shouted. "It's so jiggly, it makes you giggly!"

Then they all started laughing way too hard.

"Who wants some Jiggly right now?" asked the parents.

"I do!" shouted the kids.

Then the whole family dug into a big bowl of Jiggly as if none of them had eaten in weeks.

The lights came back on.

Man, that commercial was lame.

You Snooze, You Lose

"Round one of the Brain Games is about general knowledge," announced Dr. Carbles. "Representing Ella Mentry School will be two members of their gifted and talented program, A.J. and Andrea."

My parents and Andrea's parents clapped their hands.

"And representing Dirk School will be

Morgan Brocklebank and Tommy Smith."

The whole audience erupted in applause like they had just won the Super Bowl. That kid Tommy looked like a real doofus.

Miss Brown attached little microphones to my shirt and Andrea's shirt and gave each of us a buzzer to hold. She told us to push the button if we were able to answer a question.

"You can do this," Miss Brown whispered to us. "Be quick, and be smart." Then she got off the stage.

"Is everybody ready?" asked Dr. Carbles.

"Ready!" we all replied.

"Okay. Question number one," said Dr. Carbles. "Who was the first president of the United States?"

Any dumbhead knows that.

Bzzzzzz!

I pushed the button on my buzzer, but Morgan Brocklebank buzzed in first.

"George Washington!" she shouted.

"Right!" said Dr. Carbles. "That's ten points for Dirk School."

"I knew that," Andrea whispered to me.

"Well, hit your buzzer!" I whispered back at her.

"Question two," said Dr. Carbles. "In what year—"

Bzzzzzz!

"1776!" shouted Morgan Brocklebank.

"That's right!" said Dr. Carbles. "Ten

more points for Dirk."

"What?! That's not fair!" I complained. "We didn't even get the chance to hear the question!"

"You snooze, you lose," said Morgan Brocklebank.

That kid Tommy next to her was just standing there with his finger up his nose. He was no help at all.

"Dirk School now has twenty points, and Ella Mentry School has zero," said Dr. Carbles. "Next question. Who invented—"

Bzzzzzz!

Ha-ha! I buzzed in before Morgan Brocklebank did.

"Thomas Edison!" I shouted.

"Oh, sorry, no," said Dr. Carbles. "Thomas Edison is not correct. The question is, Who invented the Franklin stove?"

Bzzzzzz!

"Franklin!" shouted Morgan Brocklebank.

"That's right! Ten more points for Dirk School. It is now thirty to zero," said Dr. Carbles. "Next question. Name a greenhouse gas

that is flammable and comes from cow farts."

What?! What kind of a question was that?

Bzzzzzz!

"Methane!" shouted Morgan Brockle-bank. "It's very bad·for the environment."

"That's right!" said Dr. Carbles.

Methane? I never even heard of methane. How did she know that?

"The score is now forty to zero," said Dr. Carbles.

This was humiliating! Morgan Brockle-bank kept answering all the questions right. Those Dirk dorks were crushing us. Their parents were yelling and screaming. Nose picker Tommy was all excited about winning, as if he had anything to do with it.

"I thought you memorized the whole dictionary and the encyclopedia," I whispered to Andrea.

"I did!" she whispered back. "I know all these answers. Morgan is just faster than I am."

Andrea was useless. It looked like it was going to be up to me. I tightened my grip on the buzzer. There was no way I was going to let Morgan Brocklebank and her little nose-picking buddy beat us.

"Who wrote *Little Women*?" asked Dr. Carbles.

Bzzzzzz!

"A really short lady," I shouted.

"Incorrect," said Dr. Carbles. "Why do we have tides?"

Bzzzzzz!

"My mother runs out of laundry detergent and has to buy more," I shouted.

"Sorry, tides are caused by the moon," said Dr. Carbles. "What animal—"

Bzzzzzz!

"Penguins!" I shouted.

"No, the correct answer is elephants."

"Arlo, you're getting them all wrong!" Andrea whispered to me. "Slow down! You need to wait until he finishes asking the question!"

"If I wait until he finishes asking the question, Morgan Brocklebank will beat me to the buzzer!" I told her.

"What state makes the most pencils?" asked Dr. Carbles.

Bzzzzzz!

"Pennsylvania!" I shouted.

"Wrong. Who developed the Dewey decimal system?"

Bzzzzzz!

"Mr. Decimal," I shouted.

"Oh, so close," said Dr. Carbles. "It was Mr. Dewey. Nice try. And now it's time for our final question. What was Shakespeare's first name?"

Bzzzzzz!

"William!" Andrea shouted.

"That's right!" said Dr. Carbles. "That's ten points for Ella Mentry School."

"It's about time!" I told Andrea.

Round one was over. I put down my buzzer. My hand was all sweaty.

"The score is a hundred points for Dirk School and ten points for Ella Mentry School," announced Dr. Carbles.

Bummer in the summer! It was the

worst moment of my life. Morgan Brockle-bank sneered at me from across the stage and mouthed the words *"in your face!"*

"We lost because of you!" I told Andrea. "Why didn't you hit your buzzer?"

"No, we lost because of *you*, Arlo!" Andrea told me. "You need to think before you give an answer."

"You probably don't even want to go to PizzaWorld."

"I do too!"

We went back and forth like that for a while. Then Miss Brown climbed up on the stage. She put her arms around both of us.

"Calm down," she said. "Anybody can

answer silly trivia questions. It takes cre-ativity to win the Brain Games. We still have plenty of time to catch up."

"It's time for us to move to round two," said Dr. Carbles.

Carry That Weight

Round two would be worth a hundred points, and it was winner take all. We were going to compete to see which team's bridge could support the most weight.

Miss Brown helped us all carry the Bridge of Love out onto the stage. Then we watched as the Dirk kids brought out their bridge.

"Look at that!" Ryan said. "Their bridge is amazing!"

He was right. The Dirk bridge was ten times bigger than the Bridge of Love. Our bridge was sort of like a plain old plank that you would put across a little stream. Their bridge looked like a real bridge that you could drive a car over. They even decorated it with little road signs.

"Oh no, we're finished," moaned Alexia. "We might as well just give up now."

"Think positive!" Miss Brown told us. "It doesn't matter which bridge looks better. The only thing that matters is how much weight it can support."

Dr. Carbles walked around the stage,

looking at both bridges. Then he asked us to tell the audience what materials we used to build them.

"We made our bridge out of toothpicks," said Neil the nude kid.

"We made our bridge out of match-sticks," said Morgan Brocklebank.

"Very creative!" said Dr. Carbles. "Now it's time to see which bridge is stronger."

Some big guys who looked like weight lifters came out carrying a bunch of bar-bells. They lined them up across the stage.

Dr. Carbles told them to put the lightest barbell on the Dirk bridge. Then he told them to take the barbell off and put it on the Bridge of Love.

"Both bridges easily support twenty pounds," Dr. Carbles announced. "Very good. Let's see if they can handle thirty pounds."

The weight lifters put the next barbell on the Dirk bridge. Then they put it on the Bridge of Love. Neither of the bridges collapsed.

"Both bridges can hold thirty pounds," Dr. Carbles announced. "Next?"

The weight lifters put the forty-pound barbell on, and both of the bridges were able to hold it up.

"This is when things get interesting," announced Dr. Carbles as the guys went to get the fifty-pound barbell.

I was nervous. We all were. Emily weighs fifty-one pounds, and our first bridge couldn't hold her. But when the weight lifters put the fifty-pound barbell on the Bridge of Love, it held up just fine.

"Both bridges can support fifty pounds," Dr. Carbles announced. "Let's keep going."

Sixty pounds. Seventy pounds!

Those barbells looked heavy, but both bridges were still standing.

"It's holding up!" Andrea said excitedly.

"The Bridge of Love is amazing!" said Emily.

Eighty pounds! It was so exciting! We

were all on pins and needles.

Well, not really. We were just standing there on the stage. If we had been on pins and needles, it would have hurt.

Ninety pounds!

Everybody wanted to know which bridge would win. The tension was unbearable. There was electricity in the air.

Well, not really. If there was electricity in the air, we all would have been electrocuted.

"Bring out the one-hundred-pound barbell," ordered Dr. Carbles.

The weight lifters brought out a huge barbell and carefully rested it on our little Bridge of Love.

It held up! I couldn't believe it.

Then they picked up the hundred-pound barbell and lowered it onto the Dirk bridge.

Crunch! Crash!

The bridge collapsed! Matchsticks went flying everywhere! The audience groaned.

"Ella Mentry School wins round two!" announced Dr. Carbles.

"You did it!" shouted Miss Brown.

We were all yelling and screaming and freaking out. It was the greatest moment of my life! I looked across the stage at Morgan Brocklebank and mouthed the words *"nah-nah-nah boo-boo."*

"Great job, both teams," said Dr. Carbles. "The score is now 110 to 100 in favor of Ella Mentry School. Let's move on to round three."

Talking Trash

Round three was called "Spontaneous." I had no idea what that meant, but Little Miss Know-It-All told me spontaneous means "making stuff up on the spot."

Dr. Carbles went over to speak into the microphone.

"In round three," he announced, "each

team has to write a poem . . ."

Oh no. Everybody looked at me.

"Arlo, you're good at writing poems," said Andrea.

"I am not."

Actually, I am good at writing poems. That was how I got into the gifted and talented program in the first place. I just don't like poetry.

". . . and the poem," said Dr. Carbles, "must be about garbage."

WHAT?!

Dr. Carbles said we would have two minutes to write down our poem. Miss Brown gave us a pad and a pen. We huddled together like a football team.

"Who writes poems about garbage?" whispered Ryan.

"That's a dumb topic," whispered Michael.

"What are we supposed to say about garbage?" whispered Neil.

"I don't know," whispered Emily. "We'll come up with something."

"Arlo, you need to come up with something," whispered Andrea.

"Why me?" I whispered. "Why don't *you* write a poem about garbage?"

"I don't know how to write poems," she whispered back. "That's your job!"

"We're running out of time!" whispered Alexia.

I tried to think of a poem about garbage. I was concentrating so hard that my brain hurt.

"I can't think of anything!" I said.

"Time's up!" shouted Dr. Carbles. "Okay, let's hear the garbage poems. Dirk School, you go first."

Tommy the nose picker went out to the middle of the stage holding his pad. He read his poem . . .

"Roses are red.
Pens are inky.
Perfume smells nice.
But garbage is stinky."

Everybody clapped.

"Man, that poem was lame," Ryan whispered to me. "You gotta be able to come up with something better than that, A.J."

"Wonderful, Tommy!" said Dr. Carbles. "Okay, Ella Mentry School, let's hear your garbage poem."

Ryan and Michael pushed me out to the middle of the stage. Everybody was staring at me. I didn't know what to say. I didn't know what to do. I had to think fast.

"Okay, give me a beat, you guys," I said.

Michael, Ryan, Neil, and Alexia started beatboxing.* Everybody started bobbing their heads to the beat. I closed my eyes. And then I started rapping. . . .

---

*If you don't know what that means, go to YouTube and search for "beatboxing."

"Dirt and dust and junk and ash.
Now you know I'm talkin' trash.
I know this may make you throw up,
but I think that when I grow up
I will have a secret plan
to be a well-paid garbageman.

"Other kids can be accountants.
I'll live on a garbage mountain.
It may cost a million bucks,
but I'll buy ten big garbage trucks
and drive around all day in haste
to pick up everybody's waste.

"I think garbage is quite pretty,
especially piled up in the city.
You may think that it's a handful
when they take it to the landfill.
But garbage makes me sing and jump,
especially at the garbage dump.

"I know that it will make you gag.
But I like to smell a garbage bag.
There are things that I can't do,

like run real fast or cook a stew.
I can't sing or drive a van.
But if I can't do it, garbage can!

"I'd like to make one small proposal,
while I'm here at your disposal.
Let's make Monday Garbage Day.
And Tuesday too. What do you say?
Wednesday, Thursday, Friday as well.
And Garbage Weekend would be swell.

"What would we do without Garbage Day?
We'd have nothing to throw away."

By the end of my rap, everybody was clapping with the beat. Even the Dirk parents were into it. Dr. Carbles went over to the microphone.

"And the winner of round three is . . . Ella Mentry School!"

"You did it, A.J.!" Miss Brown shouted.

We were all shrieking and hooting and hollering and freaking out. Now the score was 210–100. We were winning, big!

It was the greatest moment of my life.

Grudge Match

When we were done celebrating, those weight lifters carried a swimming pool out to the middle of the stage. Then they took a big hose and started squirting red stuff into the pool.

"Wow, where do you think they got a swimming pool?" Michael asked.

"From Rent-A-Swimming Pool," I told him. "You can rent anything."

"Round four of the Brain Games will be a surprise competition worth a hundred points," announced Dr. Carbles. "Dirk School and Ella Mentry School will compete at Jiggly wrestling!"

WHAT?! They were filling the swimming pool with Jiggly gelatin? That's crazy!

"I'm not doing that," said Andrea. "No way!"

"Me neither!" said Emily, who won't do anything Andrea won't do.

"Wait a minute," said Morgan Brockle-bank. "We have to wrestle in Jiggly gelatin?"

"No," replied Dr. Carbles. "Of course not. The principal of each school has to wrestle in Jiggly gelatin."

I looked over at Mr. Klutz. Suddenly, he was wearing a bathing suit! He climbed up on the stage and we all cheered.

"What does Jiggly wrestling have to do with using your brain?" asked Andrea.

"The Jiggly gelatin company said they would only sponsor the Brain Games if someone from each school wrestled in a pool filled with Jiggly," said Dr. Carbles. "Where is Mr. Wilson of Dirk School?"

Mr. Wilson climbed up onstage.

"I'm very sorry," he said. "But I'm allergic to Jiggly gelatin. So I won't be able to wrestle. Is there anybody who can take my place?"

All the grown-ups slinked down in their seats. That's what you do when you don't want to get called on.

"I will represent Dirk School!" shouted Dr. Carbles.

That's when the most amazing thing in the history of the world happened. Dr. Carbles took off all his clothes!

Well, he didn't take off *all* his clothes. He was wearing a bathing suit. That was weird. He must have thought he was going to go swimming today.

Dr. Carbles and Mr. Klutz turned to face each other.

"You're going to lose, Klutz!" said Dr. Carbles.

"I don't think so, Walrus Face!" said Mr. Klutz.

"Oh, snap!" said Ryan.

I remembered that the two of them didn't like each other. Back in high school, Mr. Klutz gave Dr. Carbles the nickname

Walrus Face, and then everybody called him that.

As they climbed into the swimming pool, everybody started yelling and screaming. Well, everybody but Little Miss Perfect, of course.

"This is not a good example for children," Andrea told Miss Brown. "I don't like violence."

"What do you have against violins?" I asked her.

"I think it's a *great* idea," said Miss Brown. "*Anybody* can wrestle on the floor. It takes *creativity* to wrestle in a swimming pool filled with Jiggly."

A bell rang. Mr. Klutz and Dr. Carbles

grabbed each other by the shoulders.

"Klutz! Klutz! Klutz!" we all chanted.

"Carbles! Carbles! Carbles!" chanted the Dirk crowd.

In seconds the two of them were covered with red Jiggly, flipping and flopping all over the pool. It was hilarious! We got to see it live and in person. You should have been there!

"You can do it, Mr. Klutz!" shouted Neil. "We need those hundred points!"

First it looked like Mr. Klutz was winning. Then it looked like Dr. Carbles was winning. Then it looked like Mr. Klutz was winning again. Then it looked like Dr. Carbles was winning again! It was a

seesaw battle, even though there weren't any seesaws around.*

Then Mr. Klutz pulled the toupee off Dr. Carbles's head. That got him *really* mad. He picked Mr. Klutz up, held him over his head, and threw him down into the Jiggly.

"Glug glug!" shouted Mr. Klutz. "I give up!"

Dr. Carbles raised his arms in the air.

"In your face, Klutz!" he shouted.

The Dirk crowd went crazy. Now the score was 210–200. Anybody could win.

---

*Wrestling on seesaws would be cool.

11

The Dirkmobile vs. the Death Machine

Dr. Carbles had red Jiggly dripping all over him. But he didn't care. He climbed out of the swimming pool and went right over to the microphone.

"Teachers! Students! It's time for the final round of the Brain Games," he announced. "The car challenge!"

"Ooooooooh!" everybody ooooohed.

It would all come down to this. The team that built the best car would win the Brain Games.

The weight lifters pushed the swimming pool out of the way. Then they set up a maze on the stage with walls that we would have to drive our car around. Miss Brown went behind the curtain and came back out with our car.

"We call it . . . the Death Machine!" she announced.

A few of the Dirk parents clapped politely.

Then the Dirk team went behind the curtain to get their car.

"Behold!" announced Morgan Brocklebank. "The Dirkmobile!"

What?! Their car was amazing! It was almost the size of a regular car, and it had real rubber tires, glass windows, and side-view mirrors.

"Oh, man!" said Michael. "Look at that!"

"There's no way they built that car," said Ryan.

"I bet their parents did all the work," said Alexia. "It's not fair."

The audience was yelling and screaming and hooting and hollering.

"Nice car!" said Dr. Carbles. "And what do you use to power the Dirkmobile?"

"We built our own engine," Morgan Brocklebank said into the mic. "It runs on methane."

What?! Methane?

"And where did you get methane?" asked Dr. Carbles.

"From cow farts," said Morgan Brockle-bank. "This way, we keep harmful greenhouse gases out of the atmosphere."

"That's very green, and creative!" said Dr. Carbles. "Next, Ella Mentry School. What did you use to power your car?"

"A pencil sharpener," I mumbled.

"Oh, man," Ryan said. "We are finished."

"Our car is going to crush your pathetic car," said Morgan Brocklebank, "and the Dirkmobile is going to change the world."

"You should call it the Fartmobile," said Alexia.

"Oh, snap!" said Ryan.

It was our turn to go first. I would have to steer the Death Machine through the maze of walls and then drive it over the Bridge of Love.

"Are you ready?" asked Dr. Carbles.

"Yeah," I said, even though I wasn't really ready.

"You can do this, A.J.!" Miss Brown told me as she handed me the remote control.

I pushed the ON button. The car made a sound like a pencil sharpener and started moving forward. It was a few feet away from the first wall.

"Left, A.J., left!" everybody shouted.

It wasn't easy, but I steered the Death

Machine to the left. It was a few feet away from the next wall.

"Right, A.J., right!" everybody shouted.

I tried to steer the Death Machine to the right, but it wouldn't turn. It seemed to go wherever it wanted to go.

"I can't control it!" I shouted.

The Death Machine started moving back and forth really fast.

Then it started driving around in crazy circles!

Then it rammed into one of the walls!

The wall toppled over!

"Run for your lives!" yelled Neil.

The wall landed on top of the Dirk-mobile!

"Oh no!" everybody shouted.

The Dirk team ran over to push the wall off their car. It looked like it was okay.

"That's it," groaned Michael. "The Death Machine didn't make it over the Bridge of Love. We lose."

It was Dirk's turn. Since their bridge

had been destroyed, Dr. Carbles said that all they needed to do was drive their car through the maze to win.

"Watch and learn from the masters," Morgan Brocklebank told me as she picked up her remote control and pushed the ON button.

Nothing happened.

She fiddled with the remote.

"What's the matter?" asked Dr. Carbles.

"The Dirkmobile won't start," she said. "It must have been damaged when that wall fell on it."

"I'm sorry," said Dr. Carbles, "but if your car won't start, you lose this round; and the winner of the Brain Games is . . . Ella Mentry School!"

"Yay! We win!" We were all jumping up and down.

"That's not fair!" shouted Morgan Brocklebank. "They cheated! A.J. ran his car into the wall on purpose!"

"I did not," I said. "I have no control over the Death Machine."

"You're a liar!" she shouted.

At that moment, the most amazing thing in the history of the world happened.

Morgan Brocklebank grabbed my remote control out of my hands and started pushing buttons. But she must have pushed the wrong button, because the rocket on the roof of the Death Machine fired!

It flew across the stage!

And it slammed right into the back of the Dirkmobile!

We all thought that was hilarious, until something even more amazing happened.

"What's that smell?" asked Miss Brown.

"It smells like cow farts," said Dr. Carbles, wrinkling up his nose.

"It's methane!" shouted Morgan Brocklebank. "Your dumb rocket must have hit our fuel tank!"

"The Fartmobile could blow any second!" I shouted.

"Run for your lives!" shouted Neil.

Everybody was yelling and screaming and shrieking and hooting and hollering and freaking out as we ran out of the auditorium. Parents and kids were climbing all over each other to get out of there before the Fartmobile exploded. Somebody called 911, and by the time we got out on the street, the fire engines had arrived.

Luckily, Dirk School didn't burn down, and nobody was hurt. As we waited for the bus to take us back to school, Miss Brown gathered us around her.

"Congratulations," she said. "I told you we could win!"

"I'm really sorry about what happened with the Death Machine," I said to her. "It was an accident."

"Hey, anybody can build a car that runs on cow farts and drive it around a maze," she replied. "It takes creativity to ram a pencil sharpener car into a wall and make the other team attack their own car with a rocket."

* * *

Well, that's pretty much what happened at the Brain Games. I can't wait until we leave for our trip to PizzaWorld. Until then, maybe a truck full of lightbulbs will fall on Andrea's head. Maybe Miss Brown will start walking on her feet like a normal person. Maybe the Death Machine will run over Emily again. Maybe they'll start putting rocket launchers on car roofs. Maybe I'll make up more garbage poems. Maybe Tommy will stop picking his nose. Maybe Mr. Klutz will stop calling Dr. Carbles Walrus Face. Maybe they'll have seesaw wrestling at the Brain Games next year. Maybe those Dirk dorks will build a new Fartmobile.

But it won't be easy!